MARISABINA RUSSO

Under the table

GREENWILLOW BOOKS, NEW YORK

Gouache paints were used for the
full-color art. The text type is Zapf
Humanist Roman.

Printed in Hong Kong by South China
Printing Company (1988) Ltd.
First Edition
10   9   8   7   6   5   4   3   2   1

Library of Congress
Cataloging-in-Publication Data

Russo, Marisabina.
Under the table / by Marisabina Russo.
        p.   cm.
Summary: A child who loves to hide
away and play under a small table draws
pictures on the bottom of the table top.
ISBN 0-688-14602-3 (trade)
ISBN 0-688-14603-1 (lib. bdg.)
[1. Tables—Fiction.   2. Drawing—Fiction.
3. Parent and child—Fiction.]
I. Title.   PZ7.R9192Un   1997
[Fic]—dc20   96-7145   CIP   AC

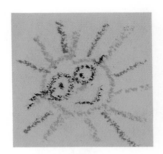

For Whitney,
with love

When there's nothing to do, I crawl under the table.

When I want to be by myself, I crawl under the table.

I can be happy, or I can be sad.

Under the table is a good place to be.

I bring my dolls
and my blanket
and books.

I bring my pillow,
my crayons, and
sometimes a cookie.

No one can fit under the table as well as I can.

I'm the smallest in my family.

I bring my box of
buttons and spools.

I bring my dominoes
and blocks. There's
hardly room for me.

My dog peeks under and wants to join me, but he's too big. He pokes his furry brown head next to mine and licks me because he's happy he's found me.

In winter it's cozy,

and in summer it's cool.

Sometimes I stretch a sheet over the table
and make myself a tent. Then I need a flashlight
so my dolls won't get scared.

And I don't come out until Mama
calls my name.

One day I pick up my black crayon and draw a face on the bottom of the table.

I write my name.

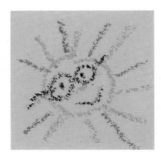

I draw a sun.

And then I use all my crayons to draw a rainbow.

I can lie on my back and look at my pictures.
Every day I draw a few more until the bottom
of the table is covered.

One day Mama and Daddy decide to move
the table.

They ask me to clean up all my stuff. My dolls,
my blanket, my pillow. My crayons, my buttons
and spools, my dominoes and books.

They turn the table
on its side.
Mama gasps and
looks at Daddy.

Daddy gasps and
looks at me.

I say "uh-oh" in a little voice no one can hear.

And right away I remember.

You're not supposed to write on the walls.

You're not supposed to write on your clothes.

And you're not supposed to write on the furniture.

Before Mama can say a word, I tell her I'm sorry.

I tell Daddy I promise I'll never do it again.

I promise and promise and promise.

I start to cry.

Then Mama and Daddy look at the bottom
of the table again.

"We love your pictures," says Daddy.

"We would love to hang them up," says Mama.

"Should we hang up the table?" asks Daddy.

I laugh.

"Paper would be easier," says Daddy.

"You could take it under the table with you," says Mama. "A nice fat pad of white paper."

I promise again. To draw on the paper and never ever on the table.

The next day Daddy brings me a pad of paper.

I slide it under the table with my blanket, my pillow,

my dolls, and my crayons.

I lie on my tummy and draw. A picture for Mama

and a picture for Daddy.

Under the table is a good place to draw.

And a good place to sleep.

And a good place to read.

I can be happy, or I can be sad.

Under the table is a good place to be.